Good As Goldie

Written and Illustrated by
Margie Palatini

Hyperion Books for Children ✤ New York

Thanks to Katherine and Anne
for their support and guidance.

❄

Visit www.hyperionchildrensbooks.com,
a part of the 🔲 GO 🔲 Network

Printed in Hong Kong.

FIRST EDITION
1 3 5 7 9 10 8 6 4 2

This book is set in 36-point Guardi.

Library of Congress Cataloging-in-Publication Data
Palatini, Margie.
Goldie/Margie Palatini—1st ed.
p. cm.
Summary: Goldie, the big sister, lists all the things she can do
that Nicholas, her baby brother, cannot.
ISBN 0-7868-0502-1 (hc.)—ISBN 0-7868-2435-2 (lib.)
[1. Sibling rivalry—Fiction. 2. Babies—Fiction. 3. Brothers and sisters—Fiction.]
I. Title.
PZ7.P1755Go 2000
[E]—dc21 99-19643

I'm Goldie. I'm **BIG**.

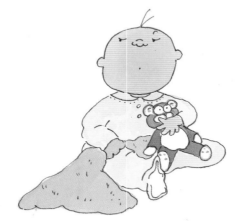

That's Nicholas.
He's little.

He's my baby brother.

Guess what?
He doesn't eat with a fork
or a spoon.

Yech!

He's a very sloppy eater.

And he can't
dress himself, either.

He doesn't know
how to put on
his socks.
Or shoes.

Or anything.

That's because he's a baby.

I'm **BIG**.

Nicholas can't
read books like me.

He's too little.

He can't do super-duper
upside-down
tricks like me.

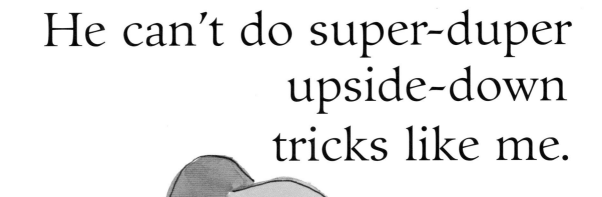

Uh-uh.

Dance?

Nope.

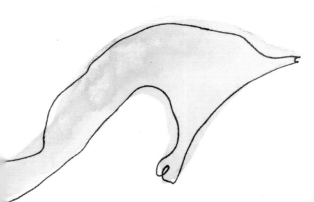

And he doesn't know how to make beautiful pictures.

He just eats my crayons and makes a **blue poopy diaper**.

I can go very fast, too. Yup!

That's because I'm so **BIG**.

Too bad for Nicholas.
He can't swing up high.

He can only drool.
And suck his thumb.

Which is the only thing he does as good as me— **Goldie**!